Hi, Dog!

FOLLETT DOUBLE SCOOP BOOKS

The Troll Family Stories
Hi, Dog!
A Dog Is Not a Troll
Go, Wendall, Go!
I Love Wheels
Etta Can Get It!
A Troll, a Truck, and a Cookie

Other series of Follett Double Scoop Books:
The Cora Cow Tales
The Adventures of Pippin

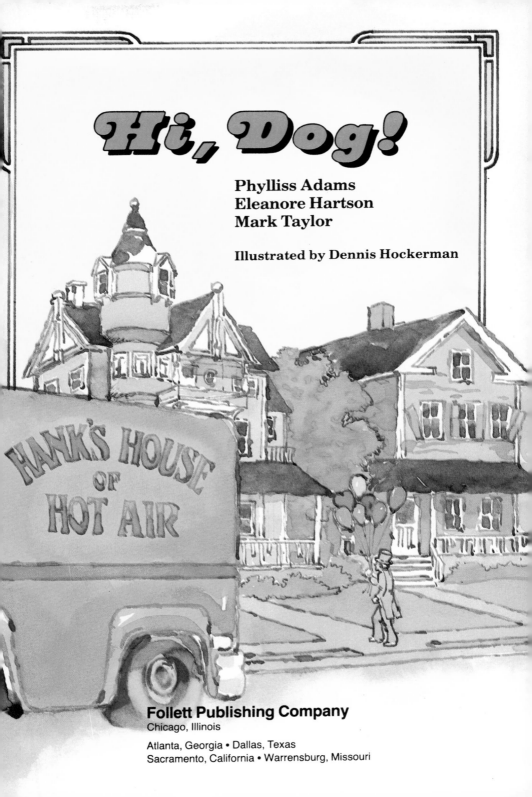

Hi, Dog!

Phylliss Adams
Eleanore Hartson
Mark Taylor

Illustrated by Dennis Hockerman

Follett Publishing Company
Chicago, Illinois

Atlanta, Georgia • Dallas, Texas
Sacramento, California • Warrensburg, Missouri

LC 81–17414
ISBN 0–695–41611–1
ISBN 0–695–31611–7 (pbk.)

"Hi, Leona.
This is for you."

5

"This is not a dog.
And I want a dog."

"Hi, Wendall.
This is for you."

"Leona and I want a dog.
And this is not a dog."

"Hi, Blossom.
This is for you."

"This is not a dog.
Leona and Wendall want a dog.
And I want a dog."

10

"Hi, Buddy.
This is for you."

"Is it a dog?
Leona and Wendall want a dog.
And Blossom and I want a dog."

"Hi, Etta.
This is for you."

"I see this is not a dog.
Leona and Wendall want a dog.
Blossom and Buddy want a dog.
And I want a dog."

"Look! Look!"

"Is it a dog?"

"It is!
See!
It is a dog!"

"Hi, dog!"

This dog is for Leona,
and Wendall,
and Blossom,
and Buddy,
and Etta!

24

The Troll Word Book

a
and

See Leona <u>and</u> <u>a</u> dog.

for
I

<u>I</u> see a dog <u>for</u> Wendall.

is
it

<u>It</u> <u>is</u> a dog.

look   <u>Look</u> at this.

not   This is <u>not</u> a dog.

see

this   I <u>see</u> <u>this</u> is a dog.

want   You <u>want</u> a dog.

you   This dog is for <u>you</u>.

27

Look for the Trolls

Look for each troll in the picture.
Find the name of each troll.

Etta

Blossom

28

Buddy

Leona

Wendall

29

To the Troll House

Trace with your finger the ways the car, trucks, and people can get to the troll house.

Hi, Dog! is the first of the Troll Family Stories for beginning readers. All words used in the story are listed here.

a	Etta	is	see
and	for	it	this
Blossom	hi	Leona	want
Buddy	I	look	Wendall
dog		not	you

About the Authors

Phylliss Adams, Eleanore Hartson, and Mark Taylor have a combined background that includes writing books for children and teachers, teaching at the elementary and university levels, and working in the areas of curriculum development, reading instruction and research, teacher training, parent education, and library and media services.

About the Illustrator

Since his graduation from Layton School of Art in Milwaukee, Wisconsin, Dennis Hockerman has concentrated primarily on art for children's books, magazines, greeting cards, and games.

The artist lives and works in his home in Mequon, Wisconsin, with his wife and two children. The children enjoyed many hours in their dad's studio watching as the Troll Family characters came to life.

32

123456789/868584838